This book belongs to:

_____

_____

_____

First published in 2009 by Walker Books Australia Pty Ltd
Locked Bag 22, Newtown, NSW 2042 Australia
2 4 6 8 10 9 7 5 3 1
© 2009 Lucy Cousins
Lucy Cousins font © 2009 Lucy Cousins
The author/illustrator has asserted her moral rights
"Maisy" audio visual series produced by King Rollo Films Ltd
for Universal Pictures International Visual Programming
Maisy™. Maisy is a registered trademark of Walker Books Ltd, London
Printed in China

National Library of Australia Cataloguing-in-Publication entry:
Cousins, Lucy.
Maisy goes to preschool / Lucy Cousins.
1st ed.
9781921150869
Maisy
For pre-school age.
823.914

www.walkerbooks.com.au

Maisy Goes to Preschool

Lucy Cousins

WALKER BOOKS
AND SUBSIDIARIES
LONDON · BOSTON · SYDNEY · AUCKLAND

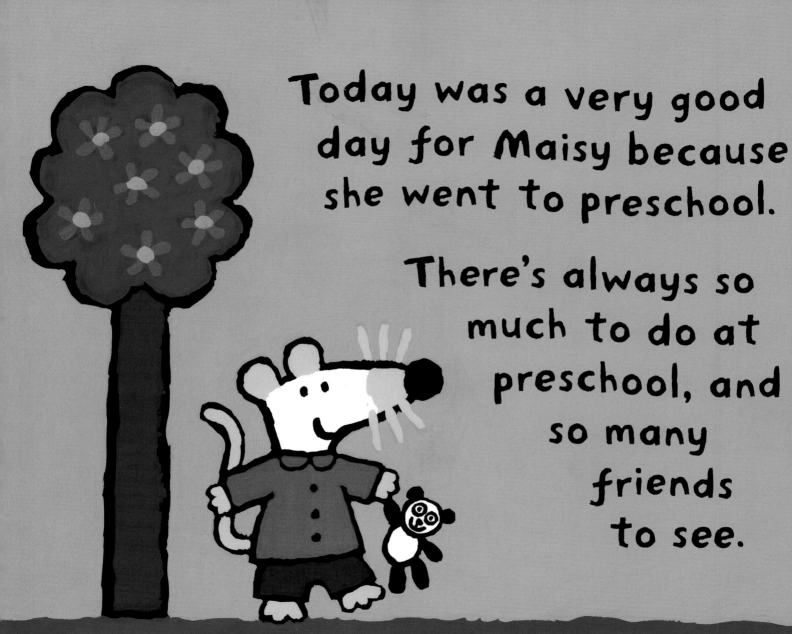

Today was a very good day for Maisy because she went to preschool.

There's always so much to do at preschool, and so many friends to see.

Tallulah

Maisy

Dotty

Cyril

First Maisy hung her coat
on her own special peg
with her name on it.

"Hello, Dotty," she said.
"Hello, Maisy," said Dotty.
"Look, Cyril must be here
too, and Tallulah."

"Good morning, Maisy and Dotty!" said Mr Peacock.

"We are starting with painting today."

"And that's Maisy and me, dancing," said Dotty.

At little lunch, they had drinks, muffins and fruit.

"Thank you very, very, very much," Tallulah said. "Oh, yummy, scrummy!"

Maisy and Dotty went to the little toilets.

Tallulah reminded them to wash their hands.

"Book time!" called
Mr Peacock.
"Gather round,
everybody."

They all sat together
and listened quietly
to the story.

"Once upon a time..."

Then it was quiet time.
Everybody fetched their
blankets and snuggled
down for a nap.

Then came a noisy time.
Maisy played the guitar.
Dotty played the drums.

Everyone played something and joined in for a singsong.

Out in the garden,
everyone got busy...

digging in the
sandpit...

playing
with a
ball...

driving the
toy car...

skipping...
dancing...

playing
on the
seesaw.

Oh, how busy they all were, until it was time to go home.

Maisy really likes preschool.

"Goodbye, Dotty. Goodbye, Maisy."
"Goodbye, Mr Peacock."

What a very
good day!